SRA
Open Court Reading

Fun for Pups

A Division of The McGraw·Hill Companies

Columbus, Ohio

SRA/McGraw-Hill

A Division of The **McGraw·Hill** *Companies*

Send all inquiries to:
SRA/McGraw-Hill
250 Old Wilson Bridge Road
Suite 310
Worthington, OH 43085

ISBN 0-02-660933-9
1 2 3 4 5 6 7 8 9 DBH 04 03 02 01 00 99

Two little pups pitching and fetching.
Two thin pups dash from a bath.

Two fat pups dumping the trash. Crash!
What a wreck!

Mom has six pups to check and catch.

Three black pups wrap up in Phil's rug.

Three fast pups tumble and run.

Six pups inch up for a hug.
Six pups lick and kiss Phil's chin.
Six pups love and have such fun.

THE ANIMAL TRACKERS

by Ellen Bari
illustrated by Sandy Rabinowitz

 HOUGHTON MIFFLIN   BOSTON

Juanita and Grandpa were playing a game they called "Animal Trackers." They were studying footprints.

Juanita could not keep her mind on the game. Grandpa was moving to an apartment.

"You see honey, I am like this hermit crab." said Grandpa. A hermit crab grows out of its house, or shell. Then it moves into a new shell. It's time for me to change my house."

"But what's going to happen to Skip?"
Juanita asked.

Pets were not welcome in Grandpa's
new apartment.

"Don't worry about Skip," said Grandpa.
"I have found him a perfect home. Let's get back to
the game for now. I will tell you all about Skip's new
family later."

Juanita tried to keep her mind on the game.

The object of "Animal Tracker" was to name the animal, and say whether they were vertebrates or invertebrates.

Vertebrates are animals that have a backbone. Invertebrates are animals without a backbone.

Grandpa had explained, "A backbone holds an animal up. It's like the metal frame of an umbrella."

Juanita knew that vertebrate footprints always came in twos or fours, like two human feet, or four cat paws.

That day she counted human footprints, dog prints, horse prints, and lots of bird prints.

Next they stopped by a pool of water near some rocks. The footprints had washed away, but there were lots of living creatures. Juanita saw clams, mussels, starfish, and hermit crabs. All these sea creatures have no backbones. They are invertebrates.

"I love the invertebrates," said Juanita, "especially all the beautiful shells." Juanita knew that many invertebrates have hard outer shells. They protect the soft bodies underneath.

Juanita suddenly felt sad again.

"But my favorite animal in the whole world is Skip—a vertebrate! How can you give him away?"

7

"I am not giving Skip away, honey. YOU are his new family!" said Grandpa.

"Yahoo," yelled Juanita, as she hugged Grandpa, her new favorite vertebrate.

Soon they would have a new place to play "Animal Trackers"—her backyard!